W9-ASR-006

For John

LONDON
Abelard-Schuman
Limited
8 King Street
W.C.2

NEW YORK
Abelard-Schuman
Limited
257 Park Avenue South
New York 10010

TORONTO
Abelard-Schuman
Canada Limited
200 Yorkland Boulevard
Toronto 425

© 1970 Frank Francis
First published 1970
Standard Book No. 200.71651.4
L.C.C.C. No. 79-118811

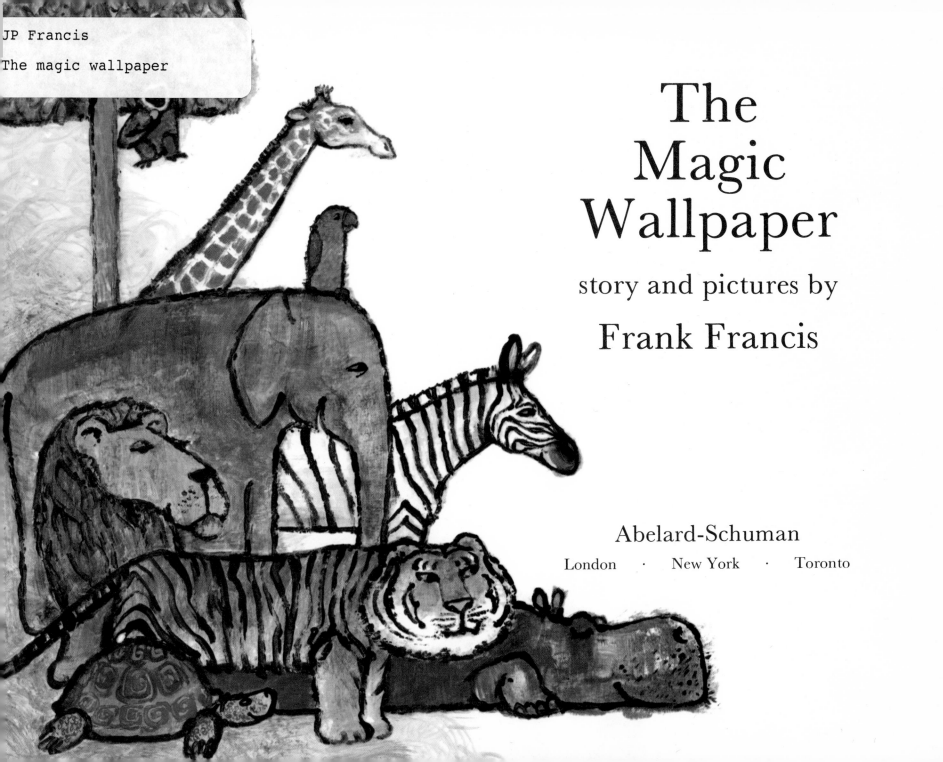

The Magic Wallpaper

story and pictures by

Frank Francis

Abelard-Schuman

London · New York · Toronto

One evening when John Robert's father came home from work, he had a parcel under his arm. It was a big, bulky parcel, in a funny kind of shape.

"This is some new wallpaper for your bedroom," he said. "When the weekend comes I will put it up."

"Can I see it now?" said John.

"No," said his father. "You must wait until it's on the wall. That's the only way to see it properly."

When Saturday came, some of the furniture was moved out of John's room. There were buckets and rags, cans of paint and brushes all over the place, and John's father began by scraping all the old paper off the walls.

The next day he pasted up the new wallpaper. When he finished, he said, "There you are, young man. You can go in now and see what you think of it."

John went in. It didn't seem like his room any more. The paint on the door and window frame was bright and shiny, and one wall looked like a forest. There were animals among the trees and some of them seemed to be peeping out.

He looked and looked and looked. It was wonderful!

That night John woke up. The moon shone brightly on his wall and there was a path through the trees.

"I wonder where it leads," he thought.

He got out of bed and walked along the path, but there were so many trees that soon he was lost and did not know what to do next. He felt very unhappy and sat down to think.

"Hello!" said a deep voice. "Is something wrong?" John looked up, and there sat a tiger. It was the one from his wallpaper! He recognized its smiling face.

"I'm lost," John said to the tiger. "Can you help me find my bed?"

"I'm sorry," said the tiger, "I don't know where your bed is, but I will help you look for it."

They set off through the forest, but the bed was nowhere to be found. John was very tired.

He lay down under a bush to rest. At the other side of the bush, a zebra stood eating grass.

"Have you seen my bed?" said John.

"Bed?" said the zebra. "What's a bed?"

"It's the thing you sleep in," said John.

"I don't sleep in a bed," the zebra said, "but if you really want to find yours, I'll take you to the lion. He is very wise and I think he will know all about beds."

The lion sat in a grassy glade. He looked very grand. "O Lion," said John, "can you help me find my bed?"

"Hmmmmm," said the lion. "You don't very often find beds

in a forest. I think we should go and talk to the giraffe. She has a very long neck and sees a great many things."

"Giraffe, have *you* seen my bed?" said John.

"No," said the giraffe, "but I am friendly with the gibbons who swing in the treetops. Let us go and ask them."

The gibbons were making a terrible noise. "No! No! No!" they said, all talking at once. "We haven't seen your bed."

One of them sat down beside John. "Coming for a swing?" he said. "Well," said John, "I don't think I can do it."

The gibbons all roared with laughter. "Can't do it?" they said. "Of course you can. *Anybody* can!"

High in the treetops, John met a parrot. "I'm looking for my bed," he said. "Have you seen it?"

"No," said the parrot, "but why don't you perch on this branch with me and sleep here?"

"Because I am a boy," said John, "and boys sleep in beds."

"Well," said the parrot, "let us fly down and talk to the hippopotamus about it."

"But I can't fly!" said John.

"Then you'd better start now," said the parrot. "Follow me."

The hippopotamus was having a nap. "Excuse me," said John, "but have you seen my bed anywhere?"

"The only bed I know is the river bed. Will that do?" said the hippopotamus.

But John said "No," and the hippopotamus took him across to the other side of the river.

A giant tortoise was sitting there. "You haven't seen my bed, I suppose?" said John.

"No," said the tortoise, "it isn't here, and I should know because I have lived here for three hundred years. If you like, though, I'll take you over the hill. I always enjoy going over the hill. I climb up slowly, as a tortoise should, then I lift up my legs and slide down the other side. It's great fun!"

At the bottom of the hill an elephant stood by a tree.

"Do you know where my bed is?" asked John.

"Of course I do!" said the elephant. "Elephants don't forget things like that."

Carefully, the elephant picked up John with his trunk. John was so tired that he fell fast asleep and didn't even remember the elephant putting him back in his bed.

In the morning he told his mother that the animals had been talking to him during the night. But she only laughed. "You must have been dreaming," she said.

"No," said John.

Printed in Great Britain by A. & M. Weston Ltd.,
South Wigston, Leicestershire

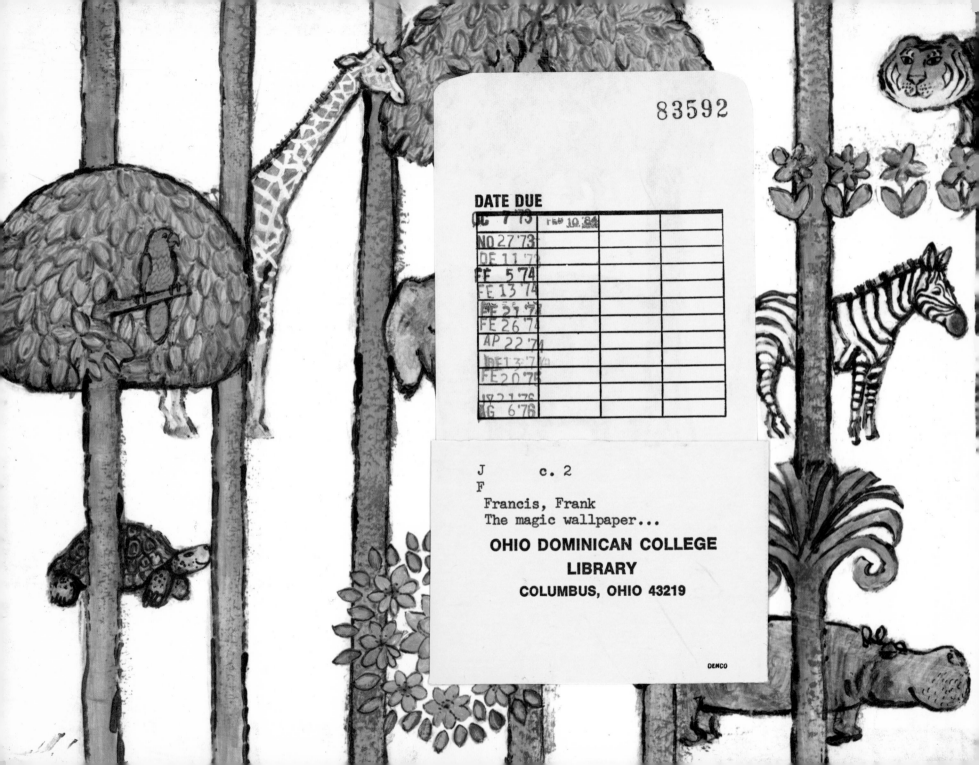